Sunrise Hill

Written by
Kathleen Long Bostrom

Illustrated by
Rick Johnson

Zonderkidz

Zonder**kidz**®

The children's group of Zondervan

www.zonderkidz.com

Sunrise Hill
Copyright © 2004 by Kathleen Long Bostrom
Illustrations copyright © 2004 by Rick Johnson

Requests for information should be addressed to:
Zonderkidz, Grand Rapids, Michigan 49530

ISBN: 0-310-70508-8

Represented by The Knight Agency, Atlanta Georgia

Editor: Gwen Ellis
Art Direction & Design: Laura M. Maitner

Printed in China

04 05 06 07/HK/4 3 2 1

To Fred Anderson, my mentor, colleague,
friend. Because of your confidence in me,
I am where I am today.

And with heartfelt gratitude to my agents Deidre
Knight, Pamela Harty, and my editor, Gwen Ellis.

–Kathleen Long Bostrom

To my God who has graciously shared with me
the joy of creation, and to Gail, my wife, and
Brywn and Lars, my children, through whom He
has blessed me with my greatest inspiration.

–Rick Johnson

*"Why do you look for the
living among the dead?
Jesus is not here!
He has risen!"*

Luke 24:5, 6

Caleb sat on the edge of the bench outside the town general store. Any minute now the train would arrive bringing his uncle Josh to town. Uncle Josh wasn't just Caleb's uncle, and he wasn't just coming to visit. He was a preacher, and he traveled to different towns helping folks build churches. He was coming to Caleb's town to do just that.

The screeching of the metal train wheels and the billows of steam as the train slowed to a stop sent Caleb's heart racing.

"There he is, Pa!" Caleb shouted as a tall man with a red beard climbed out of the passenger car.

J acob! Good to see you again." Uncle Josh shook Pa's hand. "It's been a long time." Uncle Josh bent down and ruffled Caleb's hair. "You must be Caleb," he said. "And by my guess, you'd be ten years old now."

Caleb beamed.

Uncle Josh had hardly unpacked before he wanted to get started on the new church. He wanted it finished by Easter—only three months away. Uncle Josh didn't figure he had any time to waste. So, although there was still snow on the ground, he rode his horse from farm to farm talking with folks about a new church where people could worship God. He also spent a lot of time looking for the perfect place to put the church building.

One night at supper, Pa gave the blessing. The "amen" was hardly out of his mouth when Uncle Josh announced, "I found it!"

"Found what?" Pa asked.

"The place where we're going to build our church," Uncle Josh said, a few cornbread crumbs catching in his beard. "This morning I was looking for a place to say my prayers. My horse seemed to lead me to the top of that tall hill over yonder. Then I saw it." He paused.

"Saw what?" Caleb asked.

"The sunrise," Uncle Josh whispered. "It was the most beautiful sunrise I've ever seen. It was as if all the colors God ever made came rising up out of the earth. Light was pushing through darkness until the whole sky lit up in a blaze of glory. I just knew the Lord had led me to that hilltop. That's where we're going to build us our church. Sunrise Church on Sunrise Hill."

As soon as winter began to pass, townsfolk started building the church. People got all fired up about having their own church—well, most of the folks, except for one.

"Don't need no church," said Big George, the town blacksmith. "Nonsense! All of it."

"Why does Big George say such things?" Caleb asked his ma one day.

"Well, Caleb, some folks get hurt so bad by life, they just seem to get all hard and mean." She reached over to brush the hair out of his eyes. "You see, Big George lost his ma and pa when he was just a boy. Their farmhouse burned down. George was the only one that survived."

Caleb watched Ma's eyes fill with tears. "George was raised by his aunt and uncle. They were good people, but a person don't ever get over such a loss. He blamed God for what happened."

Caleb put his arms around Ma. He couldn't imagine life without his ma and pa.

Throughout the early spring, the men cut trees, hauled logs, and sawed boards. Some of the women fixed pails of biscuits, jam, slices of ham, and pots of hot coffee. Other women sewed up curtains and banners and cushions for the inside of the church. And all the children who were old enough helped, too. When they weren't squealing and rolling down the hill, they carried buckets of nails to the workers. Their biggest job, however, was to stay out of the way of the workers.

The townsfolk spent every spare moment working on the church or talking about it. Little by little the building rose on Sunrise Hill.

With about a month to go before Easter, Sunrise Church was nearly finished. Just a few coats of paint and some cleaning up and the church would be ready for the big day. Folks could hardly wait for their first Easter in their very own church. They pulled their good clothes out of trunks where they'd been packed away for years. The general store sold yards and yards of cloth and shiny buttons as women sewed up new clothes for their youngsters.

Early Sunday morning two weeks before Easter, Caleb awoke to a loud crash and bang! Thunderstorm, he thought sleepily, and got up to close his window. The sky outside glowed a strange red. Caleb rubbed his eyes and looked again. A chill ran down his spine like a trickle of cold rain. What's happening? Better get Pa and Uncle Josh.

He hurried down the hall to Uncle Josh's room and tapped on the door. Uncle Josh called out, "What is it, Caleb?"

Caleb was too scared to speak. He pulled Uncle Josh to the window and drew back the curtain. Uncle Josh gasped.

"Caleb, quick, get your pa," he said, pulling on his britches. "Ride into town fast as you can and ring the school bell. Looks like lightning struck the church. It's on fire!"

As soon as folks heard the bell ringing they knew something was wrong. "Fire!" Caleb yelled out. "The church is on fire!"

Some people gathered blankets to smother the fire. Others carried buckets of water. When he could, Caleb rushed up Sunrise Hill to help. Surely, he thought, God wouldn't let a church burn down, especially before Easter.

But when he burst over the top of the hill he saw it was too late. The church was gone. Nothing was left but a few charred timbers and a field full of glowing ashes.

Uncle Josh was standing with a group of men, their faces and clothes smeared with soot and smoke. He was shaking hands with the men and thanking them for trying to save the church. "We're sorry, Pastor Josh," they said. He looked as if all his energy had drained right out the soles of his feet.

One by one, the folks who had built the church and then tried to save it turned and walked slowly away. Pa put his arm around Uncle Josh's shoulder. "Let's go home," he said. Uncle Josh just nodded.

The whole town was sad because of what had happened. It was as if there had been a death in the family. All the excitement of building the church was gone. People hardly spoke to each other when they met in town. When the train came with its monthly supply of new things, no one bothered to see what had come.

But worst of all was Uncle Josh. Caleb couldn't bear to see him moping around the house. Uncle Josh had put his heart and soul into building that church. Nothing anybody said or did seemed to rouse him from his sorrow.

One week before Easter, Caleb got an idea. Saturday morning he was up early and rode into town. His first stop was the blacksmith shop.

Big George looked sideways when Caleb walked in all alone. "What you want, boy?" he said. "I ain't got time to fritter away." When he raised the hammer in his hand, the muscles in his arm bulged like a sack of snakes. Clang went the hammer against the anvil.

Caleb held his hat in his hands. "I just came by to say I'm sorry," he said.

"Sorry?" Big George bellowed as the hammer came crashing down on the iron anvil. "What you got to be sorry about?"

"I'm sorry about your ma and pa," Caleb said softly.

Big George stopped and wiped his forehead with his sleeve. "That was a long time ago," he said. "Back when I was about your age. Me and God ain't been on speaking terms since. 'Sorry' ain't gonna change nothin'."

Big George turned his back on Caleb. "Nonsense, all of it." Caleb heard George mutter as he raised the hammer and brought it down on the anvil. Caleb stood watching for a while, then turned and left the blacksmith shop.

But he didn't go home right away. He had a lot of folks to visit if his special plan was going to work.

The week passed and then it was Easter morning. Caleb woke before dawn, crept down the hall to Uncle Josh's room, and knocked. "Come in," Uncle Josh said.

Caleb stepped into the room. "Happy Easter, Uncle Josh," he said, gazing around at the mess. Clothes were strewn on the bed and chair. There were heaps of papers crumpled up on the floor. Uncle Josh usually kept his room as neat as could be.

"Happy?" Uncle Josh sat up in bed and laughed softly. "Not much of a happy Easter this year."

"Uncle Josh," Caleb spoke softly, "it's Easter. Don't you reckon we ought to go to church?"

Uncle Josh choked out a pitiful laugh. "Church?" he said. "Boy, there is no church. It burned down, remember?"

"Please, Uncle Josh," Caleb said. "Please get dressed and come to church with me."

Uncle Josh shook his head as if Caleb had lost his mind, but he took the clothes Caleb handed to him.

*I*t was still very early in the morning and dark as pitch when they reached the crest of Sunrise Hill and looked out to where the church should have been. Stretching before them was nothing but blackened earth and charred bits of wood.

At that moment, the sun began to rise, as if all the colors God ever made came rising out of the earth, pushing aside the darkness as the whole sky lit up in a blaze of glory.

"I don't get it," Uncle Josh said. "It seemed so right, building this church. I felt sure it was what the Lord wanted me to do. Now I don't know. Maybe I wasn't listening hard enough to God."

"I think you listened real good," Caleb said as they climbed down off their horses. He bent down. "Looky here," he said softly.

Caleb pushed aside a clod of blackened earth. Poking out of the soot and ashes were purple and white crocuses and yellow buttercups.

"New life, rising out of death," he said. "Isn't that what Easter is all about? Isn't it about how nothing can stop God's love from busting out into the world? Not a person. Not a fire. Not death. Not anything."

Uncle Josh put his arm around Caleb and chuckled. "Hey," he said, ruffling his hair. "Who's the preacher here, anyway?"

"There's more," Caleb said, pointing down Sunrise Hill.

ncle Josh stood up. "Oh, my!" he said. Coming up the hill in all directions were folks on horses, in wagons, in carriages, or just walking. Some were dressed in their Easter finery; others were in their work clothes. The whole town was coming to church.

Uncle Josh stood there with a grin so big his face looked about to split. "You have something to do with this, boy?"

Caleb just smiled.

Seeing all the people standing there in the ashes of the church seemed to do something to Uncle Josh. He raised his arms, his face lit up inside and out, and he shouted so everyone could hear, "Hallelujah, folks! It's Easter! Jesus is alive! The sun has risen and so has the Son of God!"

"Amen!" the people called back.

That got him started. He began pacing back and forth, right about where the pulpit would have been.

"Now, those first believers didn't have a church," he said. "But did that stop them?"

"No!" everyone shouted.

"On Easter morning, they found an empty grave, just like we came here today and found an empty hillside. Did that stop them?"

"No!" everyone shouted again.

Uncle Josh went on. "Now, I have to confess to all of you, I was mighty depressed when the church burned down. I wondered if somehow I'd missed what God wanted me to do. But I found out that we don't need a building to have a church. We are the church, because we believe. And Jesus Christ has risen and lives forever whether we have a church building or not!"

"Hallelujah!" the people shouted.

Just then there was a movement at the back of the crowd. A tall, broad-shouldered man moved out of the shadows. People stepped aside to let Big George pass. He walked straight up to Uncle Josh and handed him a rumpled package all tied up in brown paper and string. "Go ahead, Pastor, open it," Big George said. "This is a church service, ain't it? Well, here's my Easter offering."

People strained to see as Uncle Josh pulled at the string and ripped off the paper. There in his hands was a shiny iron cross, made of huge nails Big George had pulled from the burned timbers of the old church. "For the new church," Big George mumbled.

"For the new church!" Uncle Josh shouted and raised the cross of nails over his head. Everyone cheered.

Uncle Josh led the people in a few songs and closed the service in prayer. The service was over. People gathered up their children and the blankets they had been sitting on. "Christ is risen!" they said, hugging one another.

Caleb saw Big George turn to leave. He ran over to the big blacksmith. "Hey!" Big George stopped. "That was a right nice thing you done, making that cross," Caleb said.

"Ah, it ain't much," Big George answered.

"Does this mean you and God are speaking again?" Caleb blurted out.

Big George put his hat on, then reached over and shook Caleb's hand. "Nonsense, all of it," he said, but this time he said it with a big smile.

Caleb watched as Big George jumped on his horse and started to ride away. Caleb called, "Happy Easter, Big George. Christ is risen!"

Big George said softly, "Happy Easter, Caleb. He is risen, indeed."